Reader 2

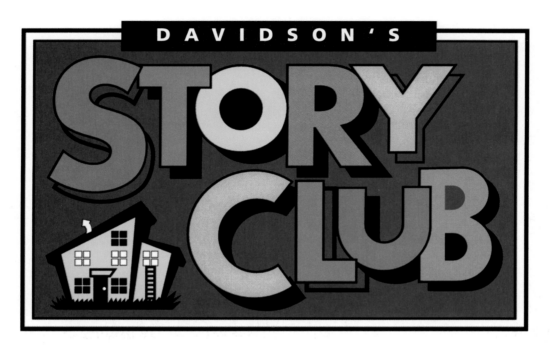

DAVIDSON'S

STORY CLUB

Multicultural Folktales
from Around the World

Addison-Wesley Publishing Company

Reading, Massachusetts • Menlo Park, California • New York
Don Mills, Ontario • Wokingham, England • Amsterdam • Bonn
Sydney • Singapore • Tokyo • Madrid • San Juan • Paris
Seoul • Milan • Mexico City • Taipei

A Publication of the ESL Publishing Group

PRODUCT DEVELOPMENT DIRECTOR: Judith M. Bittinger
EXECUTIVE EDITOR: Elinor Chamas
EDITORIAL DEVELOPMENT: Clare Siska
PRODUCTION/MANUFACTURING: James W. Gibbons
COVER, INTERIOR DESIGN, AND PRODUCTION: Marshall Henrichs

Leslie House retold all stories for *Story Club*.
Ruth Stotter provided background research and authentication for the folktales.
Content Writers: Rymel Design Group and Barbara DeWitt
Graphic Design and Illustrations:

Two of Everything	Janis Eto, Bonnie Bright
Stone Soup	Carol Carpenter, Bonnie Bright
Why the Sky is Far from the Ground	Hawkin Chan
Anansi and His Visitor	Ben Harrison, Sulynn Chee, Bonnie Bright
Trading Places	Sulynn Chee, Bonnie Bright
Rabbit on the Moon	Janis Eto, Luke Anderson
Wombat Stew	Carol Carpenter, Bonnie Bright

Contents

Two of Everything

One day,
Mr. and Mrs.
Chang were
working in the
fields when
they found an
old cooking pot.

2

Mr. Chang was very pleased with the pot
and began to clean it right away.

As he scrubbed, Mr. Chang dropped a sponge into the pot. And when he reached inside, he found two sponges exactly the same.

Mr. Chang called Mrs. Chang. Then he dropped two spoons into the pot and he pulled out four.

Mr. Chang laughed and shouted. He dropped
three apples in the pot. Mrs. Chang pulled
out six.

Mrs. Chang dropped five coins into the pot and Mr. Chang pulled out ten.

Baby Chang was so excited that she dropped her doll into the pot. She was just about to pull it out again when...

Baby Chang fell in.

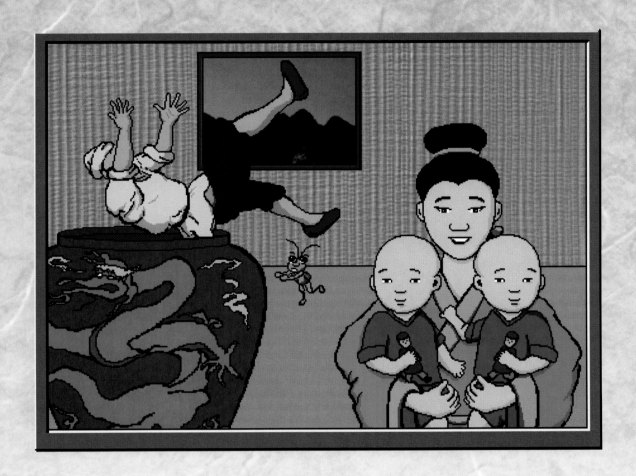

Mrs. Chang shrieked and pulled out Baby One and Baby Two. Mr. Chang fainted, and then he fell into the pot.

And then there were two Mr. Changs,
two Baby Changs, and one Mrs. Chang
who didn't know what to do.

Mrs. Chang thought, and thought again, and finally she jumped into the pot. And two Mrs. Changs jumped back out.

Now there were two Chang families that were exactly the same.

The two families got all of their coins and dropped them into the pot. First, 25 coins went in.

And 50 coins came
out. Then 50 coins
went into the pot and
100 coins came out.

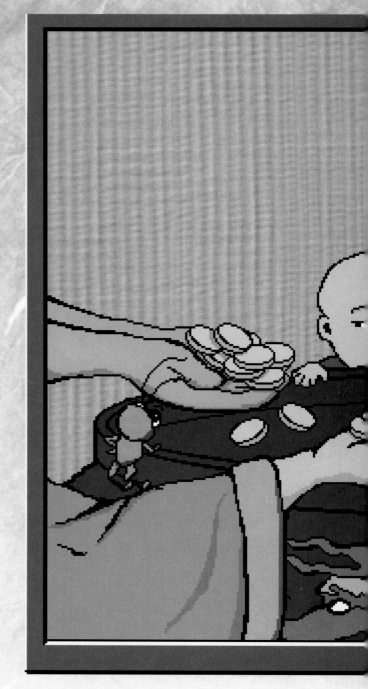

16

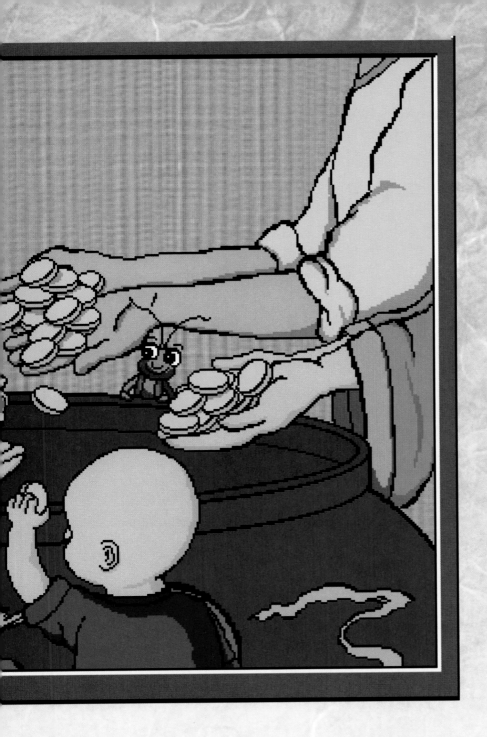

The two Chang families were very happy,
because two Chang families are twice as
happy as one.

Stone Soup

Once there was a town where the people were so selfish that they never shared anything with anyone.

Then one day, a stranger came to town
and invited everyone to share her special
stone soup.

Nobody had ever heard of stone soup before.
Everyone watched as the stranger dropped
the stone into the pot.

She stirred and stirred and finally said that the soup was ready. She only wished that she had some carrots to make the soup taste even better.

Soon the mayor of the town appeared with two
carrots from her garden, and she put them in
the soup.

The mayor tasted the soup and decided it would taste even better if someone added some potatoes.

Soon the fire chief appeared with some potatoes from her garden, and she put them in the soup.

The fire chief and the mayor tasted the soup.
Both agreed that it would be a good idea to
add some meat.

Soon the police officer appeared with
some meat from his kitchen, and he put it
in the soup.

The soup smelled
so good that
everyone wanted
to add something
to the cooking pot.

When the soup was ready, everybody had a
bowl. They thanked the stranger for using
her magic stone to make such a special dish.

Then they did something they had never done—
the whole town had a party and danced and
sang all night long.

And when the stranger left the next day,
the villagers invited her to come back
and visit them again.

The stranger gave her new friends the magic stone, but she had really given them much, much more.

Why the Sky is Far from the Ground

A long time
ago, the sky
was very close
to the ground.
People could
reach right up
and touch it.

In fact, people could eat the sky. It tasted good and the sky didn't mind at all.

Everything was fine for a long, long time,
until one day the sky noticed that people
were taking more than they needed.

Sometimes they forgot to say "Please" or
"Thank you" or even "How do you do?"
before they took a piece to eat.

42

Finally, the sky spoke up and told the people to be more careful about how they used him.

From that moment on, people were very
careful with the sky and with everything
growing below the sky too.

44

Everything would have been just fine except for
Old Yellow Dog—the greediest dog around.

Old Yellow Dog never listened to anybody and always took too much of everything.

One evening, when everybody was relaxing, Old Yellow Dog jumped up and grabbed a big piece of the sky. And guess what he did!

He sniffed it and scratched it and licked
it and then—that Old Yellow Dog just
walked away.

The sky got so mad that he pulled himself up
and moved far away from the people and
refused to come back down.

So now people look up at the sky and only
dream of how it would be if the sky were so
close to the ground that you could touch it.

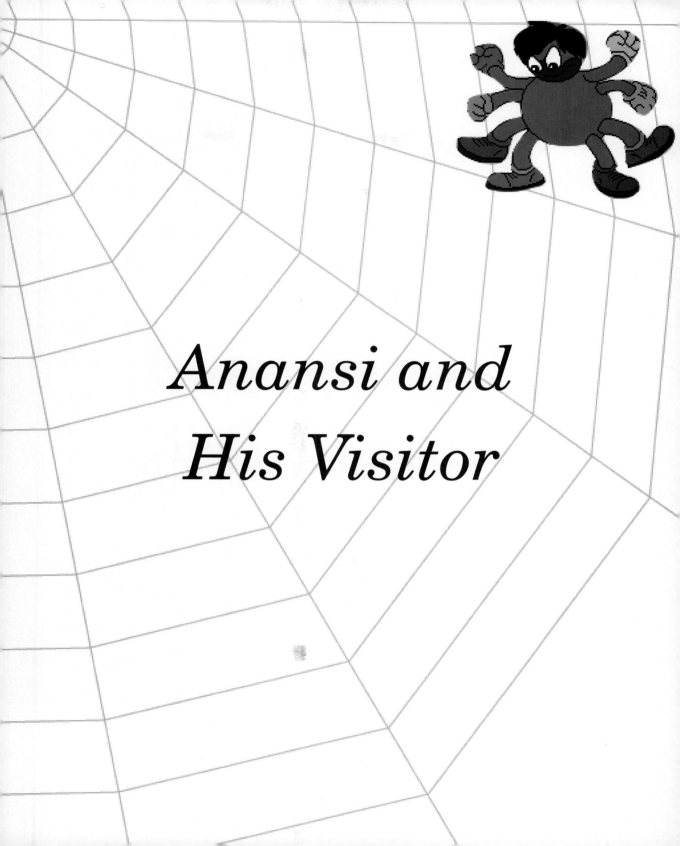

Anansi and

His Visitor

One day, Anansi was just
about to sit down to dinner
when he looked out his
window and saw a hungry
turtle staring back at him.

Greedy Anansi knew that he should invite
Turtle to share his food. And he did, but he
had a trick in mind.

Turtle's mouth was watering as he reached for
a tasty mango. But Anansi stopped him and
told him to wash his hands.

Turtle crawled down to the river, washed his
hands, and slowly crawled back up the dirt
path to Anansi's house.

Turtle had just sat down, when Anansi hopped
up and told him to wash again.

Once again Turtle washed up in the river,
but this time he was careful to return on
the grass.

Greedy Anansi had tricked poor Turtle and eaten every bite. As for Turtle, he politely went on his way.

But my story goes on. One day when Anansi the Spider was tired and hungry after a long trip, who do you think he saw? That's right—Turtle.

61

Turtle invited Anansi to share his dinner.
Now, Turtle's table was under water.
What would Anansi do?

He filled his pocket with as many stones
as he could find, pulled himself to the pond,
and jumped in.

Anansi sank down and down and down,
until he arrived at Turtle's table.

Anansi was happy as a clam and ready to eat, when Turtle asked him to take his jacket off. Well, it was the polite thing to do.

Without thinking, Anansi took off the jacket and began to float up and up and up—right to the top of the water.

No matter how hard he tried, Anansi couldn't get back down to the table filled with food.

Well, Anansi the Spider learned his lesson that day. So the next time Turtle came Anansi's way...

Anansi the Spider invited Turtle inside,
and this time there were no tricks.

70

Trading Places

Once there was a village
where the children
complained about everything
their parents did.
The children believed
things would be better
if they were in charge.

The children complained so much that
finally, the parents agreed to trade places
with them for one day.

The next morning, the children had to wake
up very early. Their parents were crying
for breakfast.

Little Anders tried to make oatmeal for his mother, but she refused to eat a single bite and had chocolate cake instead.

After breakfast, the parents skipped off
to school and the children went to work
in the village.

Hannah's job was mayor of the village. She was surprised to see all the papers on her desk. And there was a room full of angry people waiting to see her.

Poor Hannah couldn't read many of the papers.
After all, she was only in the first grade.

Anders was the banker and he had problems, too. Anders could count very well, but he had trouble adding and subtracting.

Police Chief Kristin could read the books at school, but her job seemed very confusing.

As the day passed, people all over town were very unhappy. The telephones broke, and nobody knew how to fix them.

And the only food at the restaurant was
peanut butter and jelly sandwiches.

By the end of the day, the children were so
tired that they could hardly talk as they
walked home.

But when they got home, there was no hot
dinner made, there was no snack for them
to eat, and the grown-ups were playing
in the yard!

The children begged the grown-ups of the village to trade places again.

So the very next day, the children went back
to being children, and the grown-ups went off
to do their grown-up jobs.

A few weeks later, the parents asked to trade places again. This time, the children just smiled and sent them off to work.

90

Rabbit
on the Moon

A long time ago, deep in the forest, lived all kinds of animals. And the kindest one of all was the little rabbit.

One day when the animals were busy
gathering food, a poor, tired beggar wandered
by and asked each one for food and water.

First he called out to the fox, but the fox was
very busy and ran into the forest to hunt.

Next, the old man asked the monkey to share
one of the mangoes he was gathering.

The monkey threw the old man a mango,
but he never said a word of greeting.

Then the poor man
met Rabbit and
asked for water.
Rabbit disappeared
down his rabbit hole.

When Rabbit popped up again, he gave the old man all the food he had in his little house.

Suddenly with a whoosh and a thunder, the poor, tired beggar changed and became the great and powerful Shakra.

Rabbit couldn't believe his eyes. Shakra
pulled up a mountain and used it like a
pen to draw a picture on the moon.
Can you guess what it was?

The monkey and the fox wondered what he
could be drawing. When they looked up, they
saw a picture of Rabbit on the moon.

The next time the moon is full, try to find the picture of Rabbit on the moon. And then, remember the story of the kindest animal of them all.

Wombat Stew

One day in Australia,
a dingo dog caught a
friendly little wombat
and decided to put him
in a stew.

107

Dingo Dog howled and barked while he built the fire and filled the pot to make the stew. Poor little Wombat just watched.

The fire was ready and Dingo Dog was just
about to drop the wombat into the pot, when
someone yelled, "Stop! That's no way to make
wombat stew!"

It was Emu. She explained that wombat stew would be very tasty if she added three tickly feathers in the pot.

Dingo Dog wanted the stew to be tasty, so Emu
pulled three feathers from her tail and put
them into the pot—one, two, three.

Dingo Dog howled and stirred. He was just about to drop the wombat in, when someone yelled, "Stop! That's no way to make wombat stew!"

It was Blue-Tongued Lizard. He slid over to the
pot and explained that the wombat stew would
be delicious if he added some flies to the pot.

Dingo Dog wanted the stew to be delicious, so Blue-Tongued Lizard caught ten flies and dropped them into the pot.

Dingo Dog barked and danced. He held the wombat over the pot, but before he could drop him in, someone yelled, "Stop! That's no way to make wombat stew!"

It was the anteater, who was looking for bugs for dinner. Anteater said that the stew would be wonderful if she added bugs and ants to the pot.

Dingo Dog wanted the stew to taste
wonderful, so Anteater slurped up some ants
and dropped them into the pot. Then she
threw in some beetle bugs for flavor.

Dingo Dog lowered the wombat inch by inch. Wombat was just about to drop when all of the animals yelled, "STOP! You have to taste the stew before you drop the wombat in!"

So Emu dipped the spoon into the pot,
and Dingo Dog took a great big taste.

He howled and fell and rolled in the grass and held his tummy. "Yech! Wombat stew! Phew!"

All of the animals
picked up Wombat
and danced around
the fire. And Dingo
Dog never bothered
to make wombat stew
again!

124